TomTom Loves His Hair!

Written By Dot Gibbens

Illustrated By Karine Makartichan

2019

Outskirts Press, Inc.
http://www.outskirtspress.com

Paperback ISBN: 978-1-9772-1724-0
Hardback ISBN: 978-1-9772-1729-5

Illustrations © 2019 Karine Makartichan. All rights reserved - used with permission.

Outskirts Press and the "OP" logo are trademarks belonging to Outskirts Press, Inc.

PRINTED IN THE UNITED STATES OF AMERICA

This book is dedicated to TomTom, my youngest,
a crazy character, and inspiration for this story,
and to my mother Helene, who was always there for me
and an advocate for whatever I chose to be or do!

Hold still TomTom

NO, MAMA!!

4

Okay, TomTom.
No haircut today.

6

That night,
TomTom takes a bath.

SNIP!

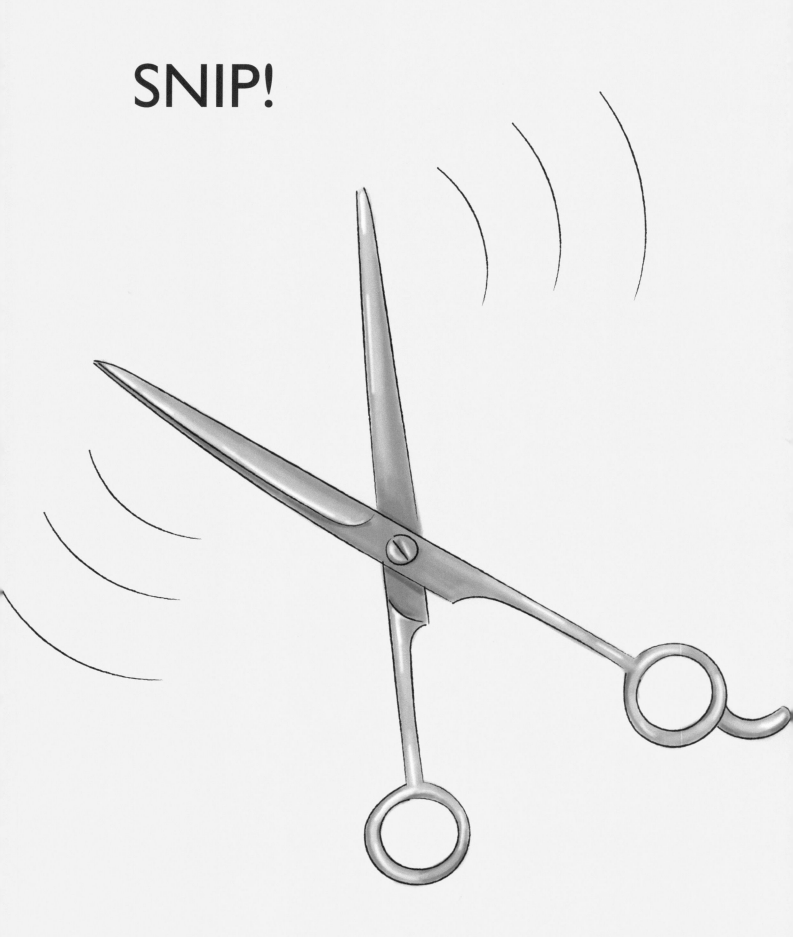

The next day, TomTom plays baseball.

SNIP!

TomTom, I can see your ear!

That afternoon, TomTom watches his favorite show.

SNIP!

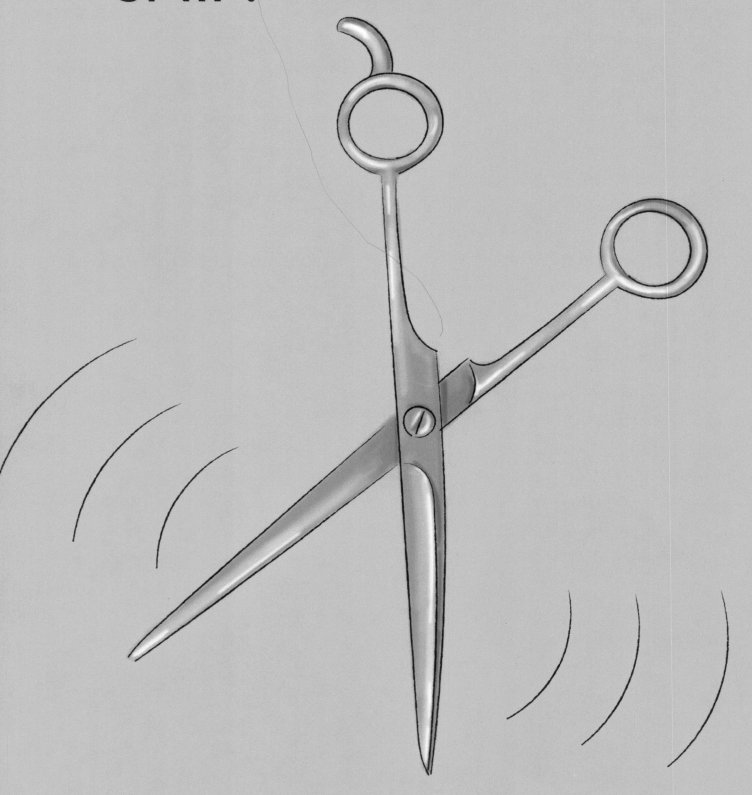

TomTom, you have two eyes!

Later that evening, TomTom plays with his green Light Saber.

16

SNIP!

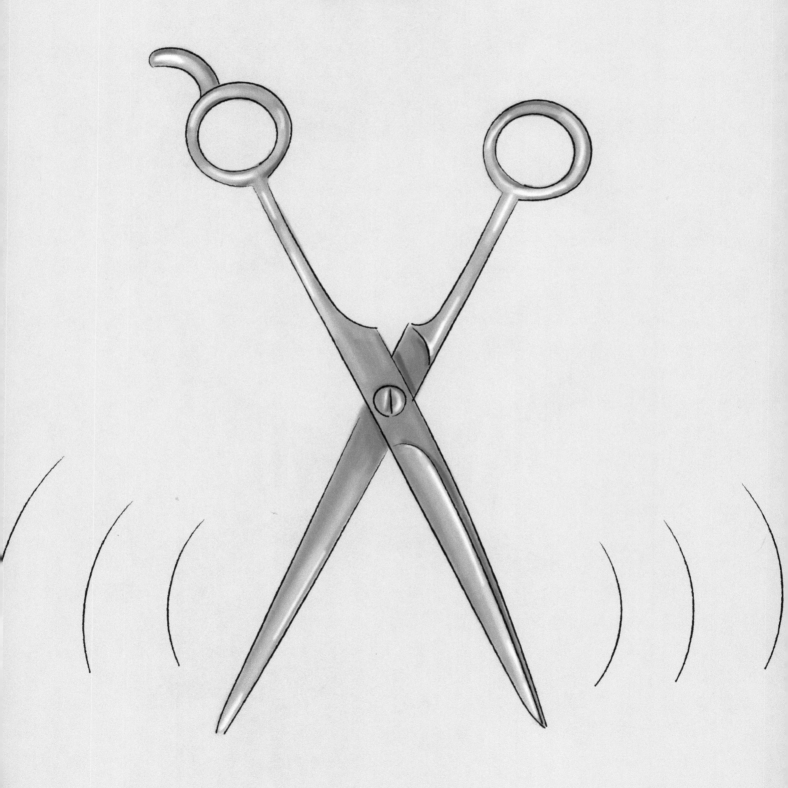

TomTom, you have two ears!

The next morning, TomTom rides his bike.

SNIP! SNIP!

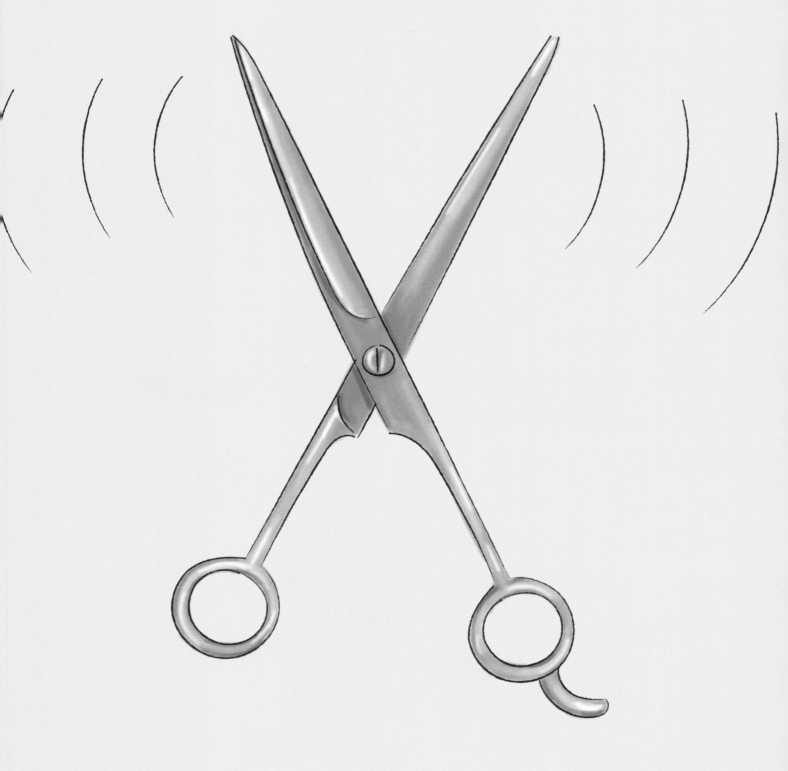

TomTom, I can see your neck!

21

TomTom Loves His Hair!!

The End

About the Author

Dot Gibbens is TomTom's mother, whose character inspired her to write her first children's book. Be on the lookout for future TomTom books, as Dot brings this crazy, zany, kid to life in her works. Dot Gibbens lives in Ventura, California with her husband Jim, and her three boys, Tyler, Tanner, and of course TomTom!

Getting a Haircut can Be Fun!

Have you ever battled with a kid to cut their hair? Like most kids, TomTom does not want to sit still long enough for a haircut. A delightful and humorous tale as Mom figures out a way to give TomTom that so needed trim. Action and adventure abound as TomTom goes through his daily activities, and then guess what? TomTom Loves His Hair!

CPSIA information can be obtained
at www.ICGtesting.com
Printed in the USA
BVHW060209231019
561794BV00001B/1/P